Dedicated to those
who help me land on my feet.

NANCY PAULSEN BOOKS
an imprint of Penguin Random House LLC
375 Hudson Street
New York, NY 10014

Nancy Paulsen Books is a registered trademark of Penguin Random House LLC.

Library of Congress Cataloging-in-Publication Data is available upon request.

Manufactured in China by RR Donnelley Asia Printing Solutions Ltd.
ISBN 9780399546198
1 3 5 7 9 10 8 6 4 2

Design by Eileen Savage.
Text set in Neutraface Slab Text.
The art for this book was made first with pencils and then with pixels.

LES & RONNIE

STEP OUT

words and pictures by
Andrew Kolb

NANCY PAULSEN BOOKS

This is Les.

This is Ronnie.

They are quite the pair.

Les is serious. Les is responsible.

Les is always on time.

Ronnie is none of
those things.

Les has a weekly
sock schedule.

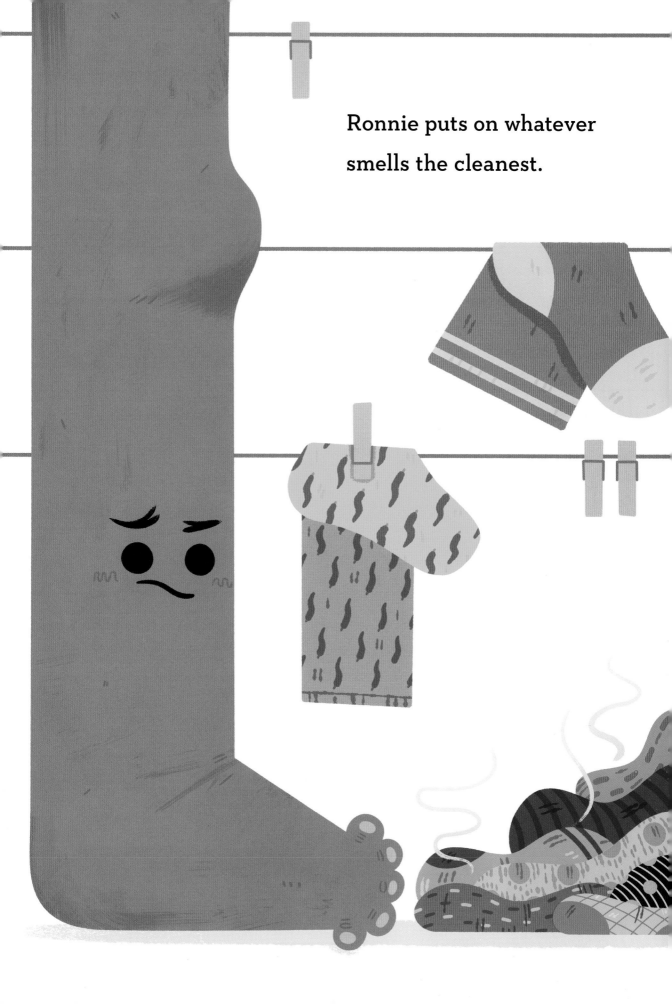

Ronnie puts on whatever smells the cleanest.

Les likes straight-laced and sensible shoes.

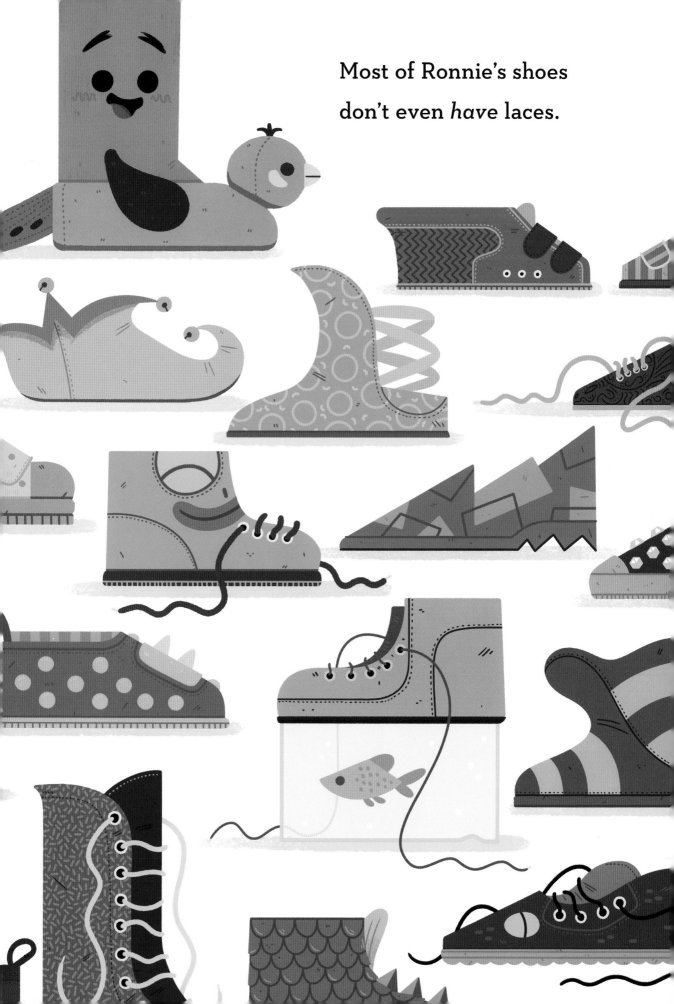

Most of Ronnie's shoes
don't even *have* laces.

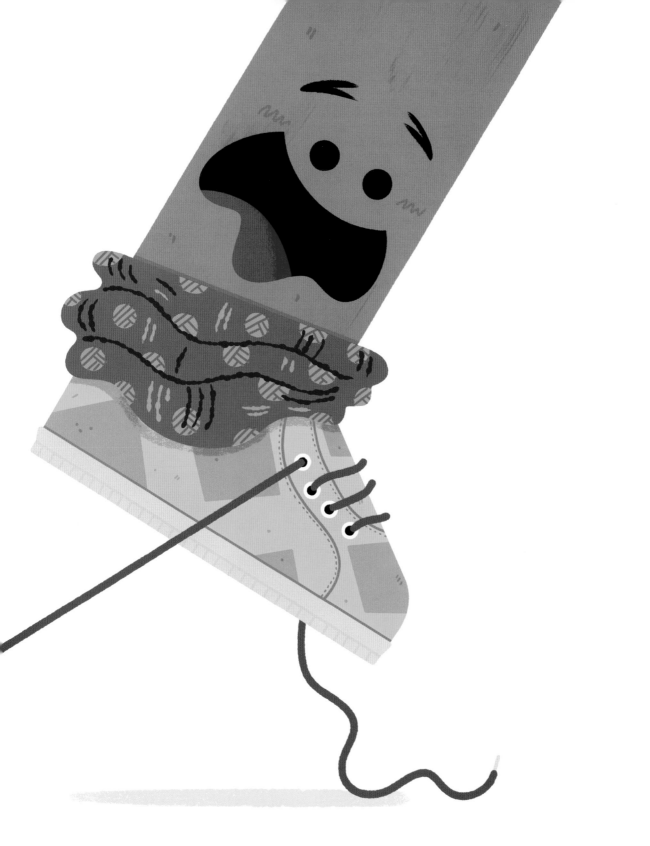

They are both so different,
and this is a problem.

When Ronnie goes dancing,
Les barely taps a toe and thinks
the music is way too loud.

When Les shows the
best way to lace a shoe,
Ronnie falls asleep.

It's all very frustrating.

Les doesn't like to try anything new,
Ronnie doesn't listen, and each digs
in a heel when it comes to the other.

And then one day,

there was an accident.

Ronnie sprained an ankle.

They were told Ronnie needed to get wrapped up. Both were scared, but the doctor promised that Ronnie would be better in no time.

Actually, Les thought things were already much better.

Now they had a routine that Ronnie had
to follow. This made Les very happy.

Both were calm.

Both were quiet.

Both were bored.

Les wanted to cheer up
Ronnie and tried all the fun
things Les could think of.

Folding laundry!

Sharpening pencils!

Even writing lists!
But Ronnie wasn't
interested in any of
Les's favorite activities.

Les started to miss Ronnie's dancing, the colorful socks, and even the shoe with the goldfish inside.

Then Les had an idea . . .

Ronnie woke up and
found Les wearing one
of Ronnie's shoes.

And if that wasn't
weird enough . . .

Les started dancing.

This wasn't just tapping toes.

This was a full-on, slightly awkward

DAnCe ExtRAVaGAnZA!

Ronnie was so happy, and Les couldn't believe how much fun it was being in someone else's shoe!

And once Ronnie got better, they found their
favorite socks, put on their finest shoes . . .

and they danced the night away together.

The end.